ABC- DECONSTRUCTING GENDER

ABC-DECONSTRUCTING GENDER

Ashley Molesso  Chess Needham

RP|KIDS
PHILADELPHIA

Running Press Kids
Hachette Book Group
1290 Avenue of the Americas, New York, NY 10104
www.runningpress.com/rpkids
@RP_Kids

Printed in China

First Edition: May 2023

Published by Running Press Kids, an imprint of Perseus Books, LLC, a subsidiary of Hachette Book Group, Inc.
The Running Press Kids name and logo are trademarks of the Hachette Book Group.

The Hachette Speakers Bureau provides a wide range of authors for speaking events.
To find out more, go to www.hachettespeakersbureau.com or call (866) 376-6591.

The publisher is not responsible for websites (or their content) that are not owned by the publisher.

Print book cover and interior design by Ashley Molesso and Chess Needham.
Creative Director: Frances J. Soo Ping Chow

Library of Congress Cataloging-in-Publication Data:
Names: Molesso, Ashley, author, illustrator. | Needham, Chess, author, illustrator. Title: ABC-Deconstructing gender /
by Ashley Molesso and Chess Needham. Other titles: A B C Deconstructing gender Description: First edition. |
New York, NY: Running Press Kids, 2023. | Audience: Ages 4-8. Identifiers: LCCN 2021059434 (print) |
LCCN 2021059435 (ebook) | ISBN 9780762481408 (hardcover) | ISBN 9780762481415 (ebook) | ISBN 9780762481880 (ebook) |
ISBN 9780762481897 (ebook) Subjects: CYAC: Sex differences—Fiction. | English language—Fiction. | Alphabet. |
LCGFT: Picture books. | Alphabet books. Classification: LCC PZ7.1.M63966 Ab 2023 (print) | LCC PZ7.1.M63966 (ebook) | DDC [E]—dc23
LC record available at https://lccn.loc.gov/2021059434
LC ebook record available at https://lccn.loc.gov/2021059435

ISBNs: 978-0-7624-8140-8 (hardcover), 978-0-7624-8141-5 (ebook),
978-0-7624-8188-0 (ebook), 978-0-7624-8189-7 (ebook)

APS

10 9 8 7 6 5 4 3 2 1

THIS BOOK IS DEDICATED TO

Everyone out there
who has found the
courage to be themselves
and to those who
have yet to!

Daryl put a bandage on Ben's leg when he got hurt. He's so **affectionate**.

Mohammad likes to do makeup and get **beautiful** with his sister.

June watches her friend Norah **courageously** climb the rock wall.

Leila and Auden **delicately** work with the flowers they picked.

Juan is humble. He worked so hard to win, but so did everyone!

Amaris is so **intelligent**.
She always works well with
her group.

Palmer smiles *joyously* when they see a new friend at the park.

David and Mei are such good friends. They are always so **kind** to each other.

Diego **lovingly** cradles his baby sibling and is so happy to be a big brother!

Jaylind helps his cousin cut vegetables for dinner, because he loves to help **nurture** his family.

Whenever Spencer needs help with their backpack, Kai steps in to help them **organize**.

Ari likes to dress up like a **queen** with his sibling.

Yuriko doesn't mind playing **roughly** with her dog.

Sage needs help pulling the kayak in from the water, so Kaylin helps. They are both so strong!

Maria feels worried about getting her shots at the doctor. Even though she cries, she is very brave and tough throughout her visit.

Raheme comforts Tarin. He's very understanding.

Matthew feels **vulnerable** for crying when he is scared, but his older sibling Ali reassures him.

Jade invites a new friend in town to the movies, and they give a **warm** smile to welcome them.

Oliver kisses his brother goodbye
when he leaves for school. XOXO!

Ira **yearns** to do ballet like their older brother when they grow up.

Z

Sanam **zips** by on her scooter.
She is the fastest in the class!